DEEP IN THE MAID

DIRTY BILLIONAIRE BOSS

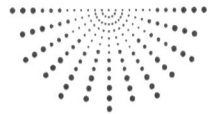

TALA MELTON

plicit Press
Erotica Fiction

GET NAUGHTY UPDATES

Click here or Visit
TalaMelton.com
for more Naughty Maid Stories

CHAPTER ONE

"*How* many days will we be gone," Melanie asked Celia, the other maid who would be going on the sailing trip aboard Antonio Reese's new yacht. Antonio was their boss, a billionaire, and every bit a playboy. His playboy tendencies were rivaled only by those of his friends.

There would be six guest guests aboard the yacht's maiden voyage, including Antonio. Celia and Melanie were charged with cleaning the cabins and the yacht's general areas and serving drinks and snacks between meals. The two of them would share a cabin, which was fine, of course, and they would be away for four days.

"Four days... Not too bad," Melanie said, making her month and two weeks in the employ of Antonio Reese very clear. She had absolutely no idea what she was in for. Celia just looked at her, thinking, "*cute!*"

Melanie wasn't naive, per se. She knew that people could be very badly behaved, especially if they're confined in closed spaces on the open ocean. What she didn't know was how badly behaved this particular group could be, given half the excuse. Yes, they were respectful to the help, also known for the duration of this trip as Melanie and Celia, but with each other, it was definitely a free for all.

The group was made up of four billionaire friends, each of them spectacularly successful in their respective fields, but all of them in businesses that had absolutely nothing to do with each other. They had been friends since college, and where most men their age had left their college days well and truly behind them, at 35, this *awesome foursome* wasn't quite done partying or pranking yet.

The other two guests, Celia guessed, would be two *females*, who would serve as onboard *eye candy* and *entertainment*, should the need arise. The four men often didn't need any further entertainment though, pranking each other, drinking, and exchanging boardroom war stories taking up enough of their time. The two females really were a *just in case* item on the agenda.

They didn't mind, either. Four days on a luxury yacht with one or two billionaires who funded your lifestyles and who you weren't *quite* dating was as good a way to spend four days as any. Antonio was attractive, too. So were Levi and Howard. Seth was the only typical *fat and obnoxious*, but his personality made up for it. In fact, without Seth, the group would not still be friends all these years later, and these trips would not be nearly half as much fun.

"Surely they're not that bad," Melanie asked.

Celia went on to tell her the standout story of these four, thus far. They had all met in Cannes, for the film festival. They had no affiliation with film, and in fact, no interest. All they were interested in was bedding starlets and models, and seeing just how much clout being a billionaire gave you in a world that really had no idea who you were.

Apparently, the clout it gave you was quite serious!

Yes, they did bed a bevy of models, mostly. This had more to do with their lavish parties thrown on the yacht they had leased for the duration of the trip. Cannes at the festival time was really a playground, provided you had the means to play, of course. Invitations weren't formal, for the most part, just word of mouth, which resulted in many people you did not know drinking your expensive alcohol, eating snacks they couldn't pronounce, and everybody just sleeping with everybody else. The hosts of these parties, which often lasted for days, usually got the first preference, and since Antonio, Levi, Howard, and Seth were the hosts, they really had the pick of the pretty crop.

And what a pretty crop it was.

Celia had gone with on this trip. And while she witnessed all the debauchery, that wasn't what was the point of the story. One of them ended up passed out in the Penthouse of the Ritz Monte Carlo with no recollection of how he got there, who he was with, or where his friends were. He was checked into the hotel as *Funtime Every Night,* and apparently, when he was getting this information from the front desk, he was told that he had checked himself in, requested the room under the assumed name himself, and he had been all alone.

Such was the nature of the elaborate pranks they played on each other. Money not being an object, there really was no limit to what the four excessively wealthy men could do to each other. But they were suckers for punishment, and they kept coming back for more, each of them determined to one-up the ringleader who had pranked them previously.

"Just how much trouble could they get into on a yacht, though," Melanie asked.

"You're not listening; they were on a yacht!" Celia said.

She left Melanie to process what this trip could be. Melanie packed, not sure if she should just pack for the four days now, or if she didn't need her own *just in case* situation bag. She really hoped that she didn't need one!

3

CHAPTER TWO

They boarded the yacht at around 9 AM on Thursday morning. This wasn't too early for any of them, especially in the week; anyone that was except for the two female passengers, who made their disdain at being woken up pre-noon very, very clear. They were excessively loud about it, so that Seth, like only Seth, could usher the pair, who were called Cass and Jada, onto the vessel faster than appropriate and forced them to take very long sips of very tall mimosas.

"Welcome aboard, I guess," Antonio said when they were all gathered on the pool deck. He wasn't big on speeches, which his friends knew, so they pressed him to make one. For a moment, he tried, thinking that if ever there was a time for a speech it was now, minutes before they embarked on the maiden voyage onboard his *brand new designed it himself* 300ft luxury yacht. But, failed by words, he simply said, "may none of you fall into the sea!"

The four friends looked at each other suspiciously. Was the game already afoot? Was this Antonio alluding to the prank already in play? They hoped not, wanting at least a day to acclimatize themselves to this new environment. Antonio had an unfair advantage, having designed the vessel himself. So they would need a minute.

Seth sat back in a large couch and grabbed a handful of pretzels. Jada and Cass sat on either side of him, listening intently to a joke he was telling Antonio. Levi and Howard explored the tri-level yacht, chose bedrooms next to one another on the same floor, and then rejoined the group on the pool deck. Antonio, a sucker for a good cliché, stood near the side of the yacht, a bottle of champagne in hand. He leaned over the edge, took a look at his guests, and cracked the bottle with a single swing.

The engines started as if by magic. The vessel was captained by an experienced sailor, John Stewart, onboard for this purpose only. He stood a tall figure in front of the steering wheel, looking out over the ocean as he maneuvered the yacht out of its dock and onto the open sea. His experience was clear.

"I thought you'd be driving this baby yourself," Levi asked.

"You don't drive a yacht," Antonio defended.

"Okay... I thought you'd be *sailing* this baby yourself!"

"Not this time. We needed the experience so that we'd be free to have fun..." The way Antonio said *fun* was very telling.

"Fun, huh..." Seth asked, laughing loudly.

Melanie watched the four interact with each other. Save for the hints at sarcasm; there was really nothing about the men that seemed menacing. The threats were subdued and playful; another thing that made her think Celia might have been exaggerating, just a little. Maybe it was her way of initiating the younger Melanie, a sort of orientation.

"It always starts innocently enough..." Celia said.

"Okay," Melanie said, responding in a way that said she didn't really believe a word Celia was saying.

Celia looked at the four men. Then she looked at Melanie.

She shook her head and went below deck to get more snacks. Melanie, a minute later, followed.

CHAPTER THREE

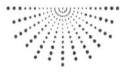

"*B*eautiful..." Antonio said, walking towards the starbird side of the boat.

"Excuse me," Melanie said.

"The boat... It's beautiful... I couldn't have imagined it any better!" He really was proud of the vessel, as if he had made it with his own two hands.

"It is magnificent," she said. "And very big!"

Antonio came up to stand next to her. He was looking out away from the sun over the ocean. He was stealing glances at Melanie from the corner of his eye. He wasn't checking her out, exactly, but Melanie was attractive, and he wouldn't be a red-blooded man if he didn't look.

She excused herself, the moment lending itself to almost awkward, and as she walked away, Antonio turned for just one more look. His eyes were on her until she disappeared out of sight, his head going places it really shouldn't. Even then, he still looked, asking himself why, in fact, it shouldn't!

He had a way of talking himself into messes with quite the same skill, if not more than he talked himself out of the same messes. Somewhere in the back of his mind, he had already marked Melanie on his list of things to do. He'd actually marked her a while back already, just not having the time to act on it.

Until now, that is...

He had been in the building when she was hired, he remembered. He remembered bumping into her in the hall as he rushed out the front door. Antonio had a very good memory for details.

He had seen her a few times around the house in the last month and a half. He remembered each encounter, even though he had never gotten her name. Antonio didn't need it.

Melanie, just out of sight, leaned away from her billionaire boss, and let her head do something it had never done before. She let herself imagine, play *what if*, for just the briefest of minutes.

"If only I were a few years younger, I'd have made a play for that," Celia said, already lighting a cigarette, peeping around the corner to where Antonio was once again looking out towards the ocean.

"Really?" Melanie asked.

Celia looked at her in a way that let her know that she could see what she was thinking. Melanie, feeling exposed, couldn't look at her now. The two of them just shared a cigarette between them and discussed the plan of action for the next couple of days. It would be easy enough, but still, they had to be clear on what was expected.

"He really is very attractive. But you must be careful not to catch feelings. That's what happened with the girl before you. Slept with him once or twice, got obsessed, and that was that. There are, of course, many stories about how it all played out, but what I know for sure is that money changed hands, and she disappeared!" Celia had a way of summarizing a story so that no questions were needed.

Melanie, unfortunately, asked a lot of questions!

8

"That's hectic. Was it just sex? Why would she suddenly become obsessed, if he didn't make promises?"

"Antonio Reese is not the *make promises* type..."

"And what type is he," Melanie asked before she could stop herself.

"He's the type of man you would do well to avoid, at least like *that*... I've seen a few young, impressionable things come and go. Not sure what he does or how he does it, but whatever and however it is, it has the power to destroy..." Again Celia summarized the point she was making perfectly.

Melanie looked at her. Her head was full, full of thoughts she'd do well not to be having, but which she was. How could she not be the thoughts planted in her head by the very person telling her not to entertain such? She was sure that Celia was warning her, even though her warnings sounded ever so slightly like a dare.

She wanted to walk back towards Antonio but didn't. She wanted to stay with Celia and hear a few stories of her boss and the maids of Christmas Past. But she had a job to do, and she had to get ready for the work she was actually hired to do. She went down to the cabin share shared with Celia and showered, dressing into her uniform, ready for whatever was required of her.

"I think you might have another problem..." Celia lit another cigarette as she walked up to Antonio.

"What now?"

"The new girl's already smitten..." She dragged long on her smoke.

"I might be mildly interested..." Antonio said, taking the lit cigarette from Celia. They both looked at where Melanie would have been standing if she was still there and if they could see around corners. "I like her," Antonio continued. "She keeps her head down, does what she has too, looks like she knows how to keep a secret!"

"You've been fooled by looks before," Celia said.

* * *

MELANIE WALKED INTO THE KITCHEN, to find out if any help was needed, and also to distract herself from the thoughts of Antonio that were really consuming her. She didn't even know why Levi and Howard equally handsome. They really were on equal footing, in terms of looks and charisma, and everything else that made men attractive. Their billionaire status didn't even come into play, she knew. It was pure physical attraction, and she just found herself most attracted to Antonio.

He did stand out. He had that far away look in his eyes that made you think he wasn't looking at you. Antonio had a way too of bringing all your attention to him and on him, with a single sentence. He was commanding without trying, effortless in his way of getting you to pay attention to nothing and nobody else but him.

The chef gave her the rather odd task of packing steaks in ziplock bags and dropping them in scalding water, "sous vide," he called it. She really didn't care what the correct term was for the almost clinical treatment of the steaks she was assigned to, happy just to have something to do that required some thinking, not too much, so that her head went somewhere else, for the moment at least.

"How long have you worked for Mr. Reese," she asked the chef when the last of the steaks were in their hot bath.

"I don't work for him... This is a once-off," came the disappointing response.

CHAPTER FOUR

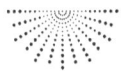

$\mathcal{T}$here was a definite sense that plans were afoot. Melanie watched the four billionaires closely. She was curious as to what prank might be played, on whom, by whom. This was a welcome segway from the mundane, serving dinner and drinks wasn't really very exciting. This Friday was going by without a glitch, save for the standard tricks played between the four, nothing too dramatic yet.

Melanie watched Antonio closer than the rest, and he was definitely watching her, so much so that he really wasn't paying any real attention to the pranking, which could have been gaining some impetus, but which he was not aware of. Primal instincts were overriding the practical joker in him.

"Are you enjoying yourself," Antonio asked her, catching her by surprise.

"I am," she answered, unsure about the question, though. Everything he said suddenly seemed loaded, laden with innuendo. It wasn't what the billionaire intended, though. He was just feeling her out.

Everything seemed to make no sense to Melanie now, just

because she was viewing the world through a lens tainted by her sudden and uncontrollable lusting after her boss.

The sun was setting over the yacht, wrapping the whole surface of the ocean in red, pink, orange, yellow, and blue. Melanie moved away from Antonio, picked up a tray for no reason and put it on the other end of the same table. Antonio watched this *no purpose at all* action, and he knew that if nothing else, Celia was right. Melanie thought he was appealing. And he could no longer hide that he thought the same of her. He walked up to her, pulled her gently away from everybody who was doing nothing in particular and walked her one floor below deck.

"Quick question," he started.

"Yes," she said, too quickly.

The two of them looked at each other, searching one another for confirmation without using words. The colors from the epic sunset outside through the glass danced off Melanie, making her appear every bit more alluring than she had in the past six weeks. She looked magnificent, almost like Antonio could taste her. She licked her lips, and suddenly he did, taste her.

His lips landed on her neck, and she moved away from him against the wall. Antonio pressed himself against her, and she immediately felt his intention, up against her thigh in a state of hardness that was anything but inconspicuous. Melanie couldn't move away from him now. She didn't want to, but still, the suddenness of the situation made no sense to her. This was everything she hoped would happen, but now that it was *actually* happening?

Antonio pressed his lips into her neck for a long moment, and then he found her mouth with his. He kissed her in a way that made kissing him back the only thing to do. It was the most natural response to this moment.

He lifted her off the ground easily, walked her towards

the cabin at the end of the hall. It was his cabin, she knew. He was just after a private place where he and Melanie could explore the possibility of what might happen. It was clear what this was already, though, so that by the time they were inside the cabin, Melanie did not object when Antonio locked the door behind them.

CHAPTER FIVE

The room was soaked in sunset. The blue-black almost light streamed into the cabin through the round glass panes lining the entire side of it, falling generously on the bed, a bed which looked made for Melanie now. Antonio lifted her, again easily, carried her to the bed and placed her down on it. He stood over her, watched her as he took off his golf shirt, his erection straining against his shorts.

Melanie fumbled with the buttons on her uniform, her hands shaking so much that she couldn't get a single one undone. She knew that this would have to be left to Antonio, something she didn't mind but wasn't sure if he did. He took his shorts off and then freed his massive meat so that it seemed to breathe a sigh of relief. Melanie looked at it for all of one second before moving her eyes to meet Antonio's.

He walked towards her, towards the bed, and Melanie moved back up on the bed. He got on the bed, not quite on top of her, trying not to be threatening. But there was no other way for her to read anything that he did now. Every move he made seemed, but wasn't, like a monumental threat.

"Are you nervous," he asked, looking down at himself.

"A little," she admitted, looking at his hardness.

Antonio lay next to her on the bed and put her hand on him. Then he set to work on her buttons while she acquainted herself with the length and girth of him. One hand moved up and down on him. Then her other hand was cupping his as exaggerated balls. All of Antonio's anatomical proportions were exaggerated.

He skillfully got her out of her uniform, all the while watching her get more and more comfortable with him. She was kissing his chest, sucking on his nipples, perfectly, as her hand moved with increased purpose on his meat. Just the one hand now, the fingers, on the other hand, holding her up, around his neck. Antonio got her bra off, and then, slowly, he removed her panties with one hand, the fingers, on the other hand, pressing gently into her nipples.

They touched each other with increasing familiarity, Antonio's experience clear, Melanie's *quick study* mentality as clear. Side by side, they faced each other but weren't looking at each other. Their eyes were on the parts of each other's bodies that had them, for the moment at least, mesmerized.

Antonio was quickly and quite completely taken by the perfection of her breasts. His hands explored the entire surface of the beautiful mounds. His fingertips danced across the surface, pulling ever so gently on her nipples before squeezing them just hard enough to pull the slightest moans from her. His hands moved up and down the length of her body, but only just, settling quite quickly back on the rises in her chest that were fueling his arousal.

Antonio was a *boobs* man!

Then she was on her back, her hands still moving up and down where he was hard, Antonio on his knees straddling Melanie's stomach. He was tall enough not to be on top of her despite the fact that he really was. He was thrusting into her hands, both firmly around his erection now, as his fingers playfully and not so playfully pulled on her nipples. There was something almost juvenile about this moment, which relaxed Melanie just that much more.

He inched up closer to her breasts, his firm thighs securing her to the bed. She lifted her head, and he placed two pillows underneath it, reading her perfectly. She opened her mouth and guided it over his thickness, pulling it down with both hands so that the trajectory was in alignment. Antonio watched as he lost inch after inch of himself to Melanie's mouth.

The young mouth weaved the kind of magic on his meat that Antonio, whenever he happened upon it, which wasn't often, really liked. He was sitting on her stomach before he caught himself, lifted himself off her just enough so as not to disturb what she was doing. Then again, he was lost, settling too comfortably on her belly with his butt cheeks. This happened one time too many so that Antonio had no choice but to dismount, lie on his back, and watch her work from this new, more predictable angle.

The predictability of the angle did nothing to diminish from the magic, though. In fact, this new position gave Melanie the control and freedom of movement needed to really go to work on him. With just her mouth, nothing but all the moving parts that made up the beautiful hole in her face, she brought Antonio to the most unexpected orgasm he'd had in a while.

Usually, he knew when. He was usually able to at least anticipate his eruptions so that at least he could stay them a little, or at least meet them head-on, but not this time. This time he was caught off guard, probably because the last thing he thought would be happening a day after they set sail was, well, this...

Antonio watched her swallow his seed. He watched, as he

pumped copious amounts of lava into her mouth, as she skillfully swallowed every drop. Not once did she remove her mouth from him. Not once did she give any signs of discomfort or disgust. Instead, she proceeded to milk him completely with her mouth, so that when, at last, her lips moved off his head, his dome was bone dry, not even a trickle.

She lay on her back, trying to quickly gather her composure, trying not to show how absolutely thrilled she was that she had succeeded at something she hadn't thought would be possible. Sucking had always been her thing. If the meat her mouth worked on was a comfortable size, she really did her best work. Antonio was excessive, but she had done it. And he had responded with the ultimate compliment, wetting the back of her throat with his load.

He moved off the bed and went to get her a drink. She let the water move around in her mouth before swallowing it. He poured himself a whiskey, which she cheekily took from him and downed in a single gulp. She needed the courage, Antonio not quite as hard as before but no less threatening. In fact, he was still more erect than not so that she knew that at any moment now he might mount her, and then the real work world begins.

After pouring both of them a second drink, he was on her. He was on top of her, making his intentions clear. He kissed her as he felt for the opening between her legs with his finger. Just the one, he searched her depths and tested just how far into herself she went. Then he added a second and a third finger, trying her limits. He knew the fit would be deliciously tight, and he couldn't keep himself from her much longer.

"I want you..." He said.

"Then, by all means, take me," she said, surprising herself again with how candidly she responded to him.

17

CHAPTER SIX

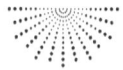

*A*ntonio was more excited than he'd have admitted out loud, to himself or anybody, but he knew that he would have to proceed with caution. He had not slept with Melanie before, and regardless of her enthusiasm, he knew that he was the definitive epitome of 'more than you could chew!'

He looked her directly in her eyes as one by one; he removed and reinserted his fingers. There was a moment where he felt like he could try for four like perhaps he should, but he didn't. Over and over, he just played inside her with the three digits until the fit was comfortable.

Then his hand was out of her, replaced quite quickly by *himself*. He didn't shove himself inside her, which is what she almost expected by his increased excitement. He got his head in her tight space and then eased himself into her as far as he would go, as far as her wetness would allow him, and then he stopped.

Again Antonio's eyes were on her, watching carefully for any hint of discomfort. There was none, clearly. If there had been, he would have stopped completely.

Instead, he was easing more himself into her now. She gave a little more, but only just. Hers was the kind of delicious resistance, the kind of sweet tightness that made men do all sorts of crazy things to possess, even just for a few hours. Antonio had her for as long as he wanted, he knew, and so he really could take his time.

Antonio pulled himself from her completely. He was rock solid again, and so it was easy for him once he had removed himself to get just his head inside her again. His hardness moved into her and through her easier, so that he had to concentrate, so as not to give her too much of himself too quickly. Half in, he stopped moving again, and then he was thrusting just this half in and out of her.

When he removed himself from her again, he put his mouth on her nipples. He kissed them, sucked them, then kissed them again. He nibbled on them ever so gently and then bit into them just a little too hard, two of his fingers sliding deep inside her again, moving steadily, drawing her closer and closer to climax. She wasn't moaning now. Melanie was panting, sweat forming on her brow and running down the side of her face the closer she got.

Their mouths met, his fingers out of her just before he was back inside her, halfway in, then three quarters. Then he was all the way inside her before he again stopped moving. She had let him all the way inside her now, and now it was up to him. There was nothing for her to do now, for the moment at least, so that it really was up to him how the next while would unfold. She held on to his arms as he propped himself up, feeding her the full length of himself over and over again in long, almost too deep strokes.

Antonio's eyes didn't move from her now as he delivered blow after blow. He was extremely gentle but extremely intrusive. It felt like he was inside of her and on top of her at the same time. It felt like he were underneath her and beside her all at once. Then he was, she felt, deep inside her, fully, completely.

"You're amazing!"

"Thank you!"

"Thank you," he said.

"No, really, thank you..." She really was more forward than she'd have like to be.

Then they were quiet again. His mouth fell on hers, his arms no longer propping him up. He was lying on top of her now as completely as he was inside her. There was no longer the sense that he could control himself. He couldn't, despite the orgasm he'd had already, something which did little to temper his current urgency.

It took him almost by surprise, almost. Antonio knew himself, though, and he knew that carnal pleasure always went one of two ways with him. He was either all control or none at all. The middle ground was never a comfortable place for him, and so he seldom played in it.

He wanted to be in her longer. He wanted nothing more than to be with her this way just a moment longer. But it seemed that he was erring on the side of no control, so for her own comfort, Antonio knew it would be best, for now, to finish up on her quickly. He needed her to finish first, though. The Cassanova in him required it.

They said nothing to each other as he fed himself into her in complete uniform strokes now, pressing himself into her with the intention of pulling from her what would be her first orgasm.

Each stroke brought her close. Only for her climax to be sent into remission by the next few strokes. He was just too thick, for her, for now. It wouldn't happen by design. It would have to happen organically. Antonio wasn't sure he could hold out that long though.

He couldn't, and in less then ten subsequent strokes, he was cumming hard, *deep inside the maid...*

It was Antonio's turn to pant now. There wasn't a dramatic end to his orgasms. There was little to no drama at their beginning or middle, either. But you were sure, as sure as he was, that he had climaxed.

"Sorry..." he said.

"Don't be..." she said, sure that she knew the reason for the apology.

He filled her, his semen warm, still flowing into her. He didn't move, making no indication that he was now or any time soon going to remove himself from her. He just lay on top of her, his now flaccid self still inside her. Melanie was sure she had spent him for the night, so that she didn't expect anything more than the eventual exit from her that would see her do the walk of shame back to her cabin, to face Celia.

"Just give me a minute..." he said, at last, his full weight on her now. She could and couldn't breathe, but it was okay. The feeling of him still inside her made her throb, sending pulses into his meat, still soft. Again, Melanie relaxed into the thought that the minute he asked for was just so that he can compose himself enough to remove himself from her so that she could leave.

And then it happened. It happened so gradually that if he wasn't now thrusting a fully resurrected erection into her, she would have thought that she was dreaming. She wasn't. He had gotten a second, perhaps a third wind, and now, now she felt in that part of her that knew that her own orgasm was now inevitable.

Melanie tried to brace herself for it. She tried to mentally prepare herself for what, physically, she could not. It would happen when it happened she knew, as did he, but he knew that now he could really make it all about her. Over and over, he went all the way inside her, almost all the way out, and then all the way inside her again. She was close again and then she wasn't. So damn close and then nothing...

CHAPTER SEVEN

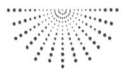

*T*he moment seemed too long. They tried ànd failed; it seemed to bring Melanie to an *end*. It wasn't for lack of trying, it really wasn't, but it just wasn't happening. Antonio really tried, but all he could contribute to their union now was his firmness.

Melanie, the frustration perhaps, perhaps just her own incredible desire to finish too as he had, twice already, but suddenly she got her own second wind. With a strength she never knew she had left inside her, she wrapped her legs around him tightly, and pulled him down onto her, before turning so that she now mounted him. He looked at her, part relief, mostly surprise.

"Let's see if this doesn't work out better," she said and proceeded to position herself on him until he was again all the way up inside her. She moved until she had made the adjustment until her body accepted him fully in this new position. Melanie made no attempts at sexy, now. It was all just about getting comfortable.

And then she was!

She moved on him with the determination he had on her. But with a deeper understanding of her own body, she guided herself over him so that he was striking the parts in her that needed to be struck in order for her to explode. Like flint on flint, ready to ignite dynamite, the sparks were almost tangible now. Now Melanie felt sure that she too would come to a magnificent close.

"Dammit..." Antonio said.

"What's the problem," Melanie asked, unable to stop now, having found that perfect rhythm of riding herself over.

" I'm close..." Antonio was already cumming hard for the third time. Again he filled her with a hot warmth that made her just that much more slippery. She was losing her battle against her own orgasm, for no reason other than that she was proving to be too hot for her billionaire boss to handle.

Melanie dug her knees into the mattress and pushed down hard, making him just that little bit deeper into her. There was no more of Antonio left even though Melanie suddenly felt that there was more space inside her. She wasn't playing anymore. There was no time for games. She was tired, he was finished, and they were either going to give up the fight or give it one more go.

She decided to give it one more solid go.

Antonio started saying something, and she put her finger on his mouth. She mouthed *Shhhh* and started to ride him hard. She knew that at any moment now, she might lose the firmness inside her. Antonio couldn't possibly maintain an erection after three orgasms. Could he?

She put her hands on his chest and pressed hard, her pelvis almost going into his. She could think of nothing else now, nothing but her own orgasm. Antonio had tried rather valiantly to get her over and had failed; she was determined not to.

And then it happened.

It was hot and heavy and hard, and Antonio's three orgasms times a thousand. There was nothing for her to do but fall in a heap on top of him, unable to move. They just lay there fused together like for a long while...

ABOUT THE AUTHOR

Tala Melton is an emerging erotica author of naughty maids and their billionaire bosses.

Readers: I want to expand a few of the stories to see where the characters can be explored further. If there are any of the stories that you would like to read more about again, I'd love to hear from you!

Visit my blog at Tala Melton Blog
Join my newsletter for free exclusive previews Tala Melton Newsletter
Follow me on Twitter at Tala Melton Twitter
Like my page on Facebook at Tala Melton FB

Sign up for Free Stories from Xplicit Press Authors
Xplicit Press Updates
Like Xplicit Press on Facebook
Follow Xplicit Press on Twitter